The Werepuppy

Jacqueline Wilson writes for children of all ages. *The Suitcase Kid* won the Children's Book Award, *Double Act* won the Smarties Prize, and *The Illustrated Mum* won the *Guardian* Children's Book of the Year Award.

Jacqueline lives near London in a small house crammed with 10,000 books.

Puffin books by Jacqueline Wilson

TAKE A GOOD LOOK
VIDEO ROSE
THE WEREPUPPY
THE WEREPUPPY ON HOLIDAY

For younger readers

MARK SPARK IN THE DARK

Jacqueline Wilson

The Werepuppy

Illustrated by Janet Robertson

PUFFIN

PUFFIN BOOKS

Published by the Penguin Group
Penguin Books Ltd, 80 Strand, London WC2R 0RL, England
Penguin Group (USA), Inc., 375 Hudson Street, New York, New York 10014, USA
Penguin Books Australia Ltd, 250 Camberwell Road, Camberwell,
Victoria 3124, Australia
Penguin Books Canada Ltd, 10 Alcorn Avenue, Toronto, Ontario, Canada M4V 3B2
Penguin Books India (P) Ltd, 11 Community Centre, Panchsheel Park,
New Delhi – 110 017, India
Penguin Group (NZ), cnr Airborne and Rosedale Roads, Albany,
Auckland 1310, New Zealand
Penguin Books (South Africa) (Pty) Ltd, 24 Sturdee Avenue, Rosebank 2196,
South Africa

Penguin Books Ltd, Registered Offices: 80 Strand, London WC2R 0RL, England

www.penguin.com

First published by Blackie & Son Ltd 1991
Published in Puffin Books 1993
Published in this edition 2004
11

Text copyright © Jacqueline Wilson, 1991
Illustrations copyright © Janet Robertson, 1991
Introduction copyright © Julia Eccleshare, 2004
All rights reserved

The moral right of the authors and illustrator has been asserted

Set in 14.5/17 Bembo
Made and printed in England by Clays Ltd, St Ives plc

British Library Cataloguing in Publication Data
A CIP catalogue record for this book is available from the British Library

ISBN-13: 978-0-14-131721-2

www.greenpenguin.co.uk

Mixed Sources
Product group from well-managed
forests and other controlled sources
www.fsc.org Cert no. SA-COC-1592
© 1996 Forest Stewardship Council
FSC

Penguin Books is committed to a sustainable future
for our business, our readers and our planet.
The book in your hands is made from paper
certified by the Forest Stewardship Council.

For Peter and Tumble

INTRODUCTION

by Julia Eccleshare, Series Editor

To choose the dog that bites your sister to be your new pet doesn't sound like the kind of thing a wimp would do. And that's exactly why Micky does it. What better way can he find of proving to his sister that he isn't the boy she thinks he is?

Poor old Micky. He has three sisters – two older and one younger. That would be bad enough, but what makes matters worse is that they are all tough and brave, and Micky is not. In fact, Micky is frightened of almost everything and he is particularly frightened by the werewolves video. I'm a wimp too, especially when it comes to films, so I can easily understand Micky's terror. And everyone can understand how horrible it is for him to be labelled – especially by his dad.

Mum's method of putting some backbone into Micky by getting him a puppy of his own looks in danger of backfiring, but when Micky chooses the most vicious and unpredictable grey puppy out of all the handsome pups in the dog shelter, he finds an alter ego that changes his life. Wolfie – it's a great name anyway – seems to have a special understanding with Micky. They always say that opposites attract and Wolfie's unruly habits, total disobedience and outrageous sense of fun seem absolutely delightful to Micky.

The Werepuppy is a wonderful story that's guaranteed to give all wimps courage. Jacqueline Wilson shows her typical perceptiveness about family relationships and finds an appropriately light-hearted and funny way of empowering a boy who longs for his dad to approve of him but seems always to be letting him down.

Micky lay on his tummy on the carpet, carefully colouring in his picture. His hand ached after doing all the sky but he didn't go over the lines even once. He took a darker blue felt-tip and started on the lake. He'd drawn himself standing on the green grass by the lakeside. He stared hard at the picture, wishing there was some way of stepping right inside it. He wanted to be walking through the buttercups beside the blue water. He didn't want to be here in his own living room. Not with his elder sisters, Meryl and Mandy and Mona. Certainly not with his younger sister Marigold. And especially not when Mum and Dad were going out for the evening.

'Now, are you going to be all right?' said Mum.

'Of course we are,' said Meryl. She smiled. Mandy and Mona and Marigold smiled too. Micky didn't feel a bit like smiling.

'You're in charge, Meryl. No television until you older girls have done your homework. And make sure Micky and Marigold are in bed before nine o'clock.'

'Right, Mum,' said Meryl.

'Mandy and Mona, you're to do what Meryl says too,' said Mum.

'Cheek!' said Mandy.

'We don't want her bossing us about,' said Mona.

'Now don't start quarrelling,' said Mum. 'Meryl, you will be sensible, won't you? Don't answer the door to anyone. And if there's anything at all the matter we're only down the road at Aunty Kathleen's. You've got the phone number, haven't you? Just give us a call.'

'Don't you dare make any other phone calls, though,' said Dad. 'I don't know how I'm going to pay that last phone bill. You girls are terrible, rabbit rabbit rabbit to all your friends.'

'Don't you worry about a thing,' said Meryl.

Mum looked worried all the same.

'Maybe we shouldn't leave them,' she said. 'I wish I'd asked Granny Boot to babysit now.'

'I'm fourteen, Mum! *I* can babysit,' said Meryl.

'And we're not flipping babies,' said Mona. 'Well, us three big ones aren't babies.'

'I'm not a baby either,' Micky mumbled, making little curly waves on his lake.

'I am,' said Marigold, just to be difficult. 'Yes, I'm a lickle baby.' She put on a sickening lisp and crouched down small. 'Want a bicky, Mum-Mum. Give me nice chocky bicky and I'll be a good baby.'

'No more chocolate biscuits! Do you hear that, Meryl, they're not to have anything else to eat, right?'

'Want bicky!' Marigold wailed, sticking out her bottom lip in a baby pout.

'Stop that silly nonsense. You be a good girl,' said Mum, giving her a kiss.

She turned to Micky, looking at his drawing. 'That's lovely, darling,' said Mum. 'What are all the humpy things?'

'Mountains,' said Micky.

'Oh yes,' said Mum. 'And what's the bit you're doing now? It's a river, isn't it?'

'No, it's a lake.'

'Oh, a lake, eh?' said Mum. 'And the green part is a field.'

'It's a meadow and the dark green bit is a wood.'

'There aren't any people,' said Mum.

'Yes there are,' said Micky, and he pointed to the tiny figure standing by the lake.

'Oh yes. But just one. Won't he get lonely?'

'Not a bit,' said Micky. This was a drawing of a magic land and he was the only person that lived there and he didn't even have one sister, let alone four, and it was bliss.

'Come on, Kathleen will be wondering where we've got to,' said Dad impatiently.

'Look at Micky's super drawing,' said Mum.

'Mmm,' said Dad. He didn't think much of drawing. Sometimes he didn't seem to think much of Micky either.

'Bye then, Micky,' said Mum, bending down to give him a kiss.

'Me want my bicky,' said Marigold, still making out she was a baby. She hopped about in a bunny crouch and just happened to barge straight into Micky, jogging his colouring arm. The blue lake lapped right over the little pinman Micky.

'Look what you did!' said Micky, and he pushed her back.

Marigold pushed again. Harder. Micky had to give up. Marigold was a year younger than him but she was already just as big, and a lot stronger. If they had a fight, Micky knew who would win.

'Now then,' said Mum anxiously. 'Oh, Marigold, that wasn't very nice, was it? Poor Micky's been doing that drawing for hours and now you've made him scribble on it.'

'I didn't mean to,' said Marigold, blinking her big blue eyes. 'I'm ever so sorry, Micky.'

'Let the boy fight his own battles,' said Dad. 'Come *on*.'

He put his arm round Mum and hurried her away, down the hall and out of the front door.

'Freedom!' said Meryl, making straight for the telephone.

'I thought they'd never go,' said Mandy, turning on the television. She put her feet up on the sofa, her grubby trainers on the good brocade.

'Let's have some music,' said Mona, switching on the transistor although the television was already blaring.

'Watch out,' said Micky. 'They might come

back. Mum might have forgotten something. You know what she's like.'

He was simply trying to stop them getting into trouble but they all groaned.

'We know what *you're* like, Mr Goody-goody,' said Mona, turning the music up even louder.

'My brother Micky makes me sicky,' said Marigold. 'Has his super-duper picture got a lickle scribble on it? Won't it get lonely? I know, I'll give it some friend scribbles to keep it company.' She snatched a felt-tip and scribbled all over the drawing, ruining it.

'Stop being a pain, Marigold,' said Meryl,

swiping at her little sister, but then her friend started talking on the phone and Meryl got involved in a very long conversation about some dumb boy on the bus going home from school.

Marigold really was a pain, thought Micky. She nagged at him like toothache all day long and often half the night. He couldn't ever seem to stop her. How do you stop toothache? He thought of the dentist's drill. He thought wistfully about drilling Marigold. It helped a little. He tried not to look at his spoilt picture. He knew what would happen if he did.

'Micky's going to cry!' Marigold yelled triumphantly.

'No I'm not,' said Micky gruffly.

'Yes you are, your lip's gone all quivery. I can always tell. Cry-baby, cry-baby.'

'I'm *not* crying,' said Micky furiously, wiping his eyes.

'Cheer up, little chum,' said Mandy, and she reached out and pulled Micky on to the sofa with her. 'Come and watch telly, eh?'

Micky leant against Mandy, sniffling. He didn't have a tissue. She didn't have a tissue either, but she wiped his face with the sleeve of her sweatshirt. Mandy never cared about her clothes.

She always wore scruffy old shirts and jeans and she had such short spiky sticking-up-all-over-the-place hair that lots of people thought she was a boy.

Micky liked Mandy most of all his sisters. Sometimes she seemed much more of a boy than he was. There was a chat show that he liked on the television but when Mandy said, 'Boring!' and switched channels, Micky said 'Boring!' too. Mandy switched and switched, sighing impatiently.

'There's a whole load of junk on. Let's watch my football video,' she said.

'I don't want to watch that stupid old rubbish,' Mona moaned. 'We'll have my Kylie video.'

'No, my Care Bears!' Marigold demanded. Her voice sounded odd. She had something in her mouth. Shreds of chocolate stuck to her rosy lips.

'You pig, you've had that chocolate biscuit after all,' said Mona. 'Well, I'm having one too.'

'You can't, because I had the last one, ha ha,' said Marigold.

'That's not fair,' Mona wailed.

'Pipe down you lot,' Meryl shouted. She dug in her pocket for her purse and threw it to

Mandy. 'Here, nip down to the shop and get us all some coke and crisps, eh?'

'Great!'

Mandy nipped. She came back with five cans of coke, five packets of crisps, and a new rented video as well.

'Here, I'm not paying for that too, that's not fair,' said Meryl.

'Oh go on, I've been dying to see it for ages, and it's nearly always out,' said Mandy. 'It's *Savage Snarl* – you know, that werewolf film.'

'Wow!' said Mona. 'They've all seen it in my class and they say it's fantastic. You see all these people getting ripped to bits by the werewolves.'

'Oh good,' said Marigold. 'Is there lots of blood?'

'She shouldn't see it,' Meryl called. 'It'll be too scary.'

'I *like* scary,' said Marigold. 'It's Micky who'll get nightmares.'

'No I won't,' said Micky, though he knew Marigold was right.

'Micky's not to watch,' said Meryl, but she was ringing another friend now, and she was soon so busy talking she didn't care who was watching.

Savage Snarl was the most terrifying film they

had ever seen. Even Mandy started biting her
nails when the werewolf bared its teeth and
pounced. Mona shrieked every time he started
ripping. Marigold laughed, but her voice was too
high, and she kept pulling faces. Micky held on
tight to Mandy. Most of the time he hid his face
in her bony shoulder. He shut his eyes and put
his hands over his ears, but he could still
somehow see those long pointed teeth glistening
with fresh blood, hear that terrible eerie howl.

When the film ended at long last they were all
silent for several seconds.

'Wow!' said Mona shakily.

'Good, eh?' said Mandy.

'I liked the ripping bits best,' said Marigold.

Micky said nothing at all.

'Come on, it's ever so late,' said Meryl, putting down the phone at last. 'You littles get up to bed straight away. And you, Mona. Mum and Dad

will be back soon. I'll just make one more quick phone call and then I'll be up to say goodnight.'

Meryl really wasn't too long this time and she tucked Micky under the covers and gave him a goodnight kiss just like Mum. Only she wasn't really Mum, so she couldn't stop Micky being so scared.

He huddled up beneath his duvet but it started to feel as if a huge hairy werewolf was lying on top of him. There were more werewolves crouching at every corner of his little bedroom, and another was snarling right underneath his bed. An entire savage pack of werewolves was waiting in his dreams. All night long they howled and slavered and chewed at his pyjamas.

Micky was very glad when it was time to get up. His bedroom didn't seem anywhere near as frightening in the sunlight. He sat up and examined his duvet. He peered in all four corners of his room. He hung over the edge of his bed and looked underneath it. No werewolves. Not even a tuft of fur or a fang.

He got up to go to the bathroom, having a happy little hum to himself. He was silly to get in such a state. It was only a daft old video, it wasn't *real*. It was time he grew up a bit.

He opened his bedroom door – and the werewolf pounced. It howled, it growled, it tore at Micky with its hairy hooves, it slavered all over him. Micky screamed. He screamed and screamed and screamed. And then the werewolf was batted off the top of him and he was suddenly, wonderfully in Mum's arms.

'What on earth's the matter now?' said Mum. 'What are you playing at, Marigold? And what are you doing with that furry hearthrug? You put it back in the living room this minute.'

Micky understood everything. But it was too late. He was crying like a baby and he couldn't stop.

'There now, Micky. Don't cry, pet. Come on, I know Marigold's an old tease but it was only a silly game,' said Mum, but she still held him tight, and she rocked him gently as if he really was a baby all over again.

'What's going on?' Dad demanded, coming out of the bathroom with a white shaving soap beard on his chin. One patch was tinged pink. 'What was all that silly screaming about? I thought it was someone getting murdered. I very nearly cut my throat shaving.'

'It's OK, dear. It was just Micky and Marigold,' said Mum. 'I haven't quite got to the bottom of it yet. Why were you so frightened, Micky, mm?'

'I thought she was a werewolf,' Micky wept.

'A what?' said Mum.

'Dear goodness,' said Dad in disgust. 'What's the matter with you, Micky? The only boy, yet he's the biggest girl of them all.'

He stalked back to the bathroom. Micky tried hard to stop crying and made ugly gulping noises. Mum patted him but he wriggled away this time, feeling ashamed.

'Don't take any notice of Dad. He's just feeling tetchy because he ate and drank too much last night,' Mum whispered. 'Now. What's all this about a werewolf, eh?'

Marigold was stumping back upstairs minus the rug. Mona was peering out of their bedroom door, frowning at Micky. Meryl and Mandy were standing on the landing looking at him anxiously.

Micky knew he couldn't possibly tell Mum about the werewolf film. It would get them all into trouble. So he just sniffed and gulped some more and shook his head.

'I don't know. I think maybe I was having a dream about werewolves,' he mumbled.

Marigold and Mona and Mandy and Meryl sighed with relief. Mum still looked suspicious.

'Yes, but what on earth made you dream about such a silly thing? Have you been reading some junky comic about werewolves, Micky?'

'No, Mum,' said Micky truthfully.

'Have you been watching some horror video about werewolves, is that it?'

Marigold and Mona and Mandy and Meryl held their breath.

'No, Mum,' said Micky, not quite truthfully. But it wasn't really a lie, because he hadn't been *watching*. He'd had his eyes tight shut nearly all the time.

'Well, I'm glad to hear it,' said Mum. 'Now listen, Micky. There are no such things as werewolves. They're just silly made-up creatures.'

'Mmm,' said Micky worriedly. 'But, Mum. I haven't seen a werewolf video but there *are* werewolf videos and in them you see real werewolves. They run about and bite and rip. They really do. Well, I'm sure they do, only of course I haven't ever seen them.'

Mum glanced round at Micky's four sisters.

For a moment it looked as if she knew all. But then she turned back to Micky.

'There aren't any real werewolves anywhere. They just use big dogs in those silly films. Alsatians. Like Sandy, Mr Bryan's Alsatian up the road. And you're not scared of him, are you?'

'No,' said Micky doubtfully.

He'd never been exactly fond of Sandy the Alsatian. He had a habit of crouching right down behind his fence and then growling suddenly at your ankles. It always made Micky jump a bit on his way past, going to school.

When Micky went to school that morning he crossed right over the road so he didn't have to go near Sandy the Alsatian. But even from right across the road Sandy looked much larger and fiercer than usual, and there seemed to be far more teeth springing from his jaw. He really did look remarkably like a werewolf.

'Micky's scared of a silly old dog,' Marigold chanted mockingly. She put her hand right through the fence and patted Sandy's head to show *she* wasn't scared a bit.

'Micky's sensible to keep his distance,' said Mandy, snatching Marigold's hand back. 'You should be careful with all big dogs. You never know when they can snap.'

Micky discovered that he wasn't just scared of big dogs. He was scared of quite little dogs too.

On Saturday afternoon Mum and Dad and Mona and Micky and Marigold went for a walk in the park. (Meryl was down at the shopping precinct with her friends, and Mandy had gone skateboarding.) There were lots of other families in the park. And lots of dogs. Micky managed to steer clear of most of them, suddenly rushing off round the duck-pond away from a lollopy spaniel and running like crazy when a Golden Retriever appeared on the horizon.

'You're quite a nippy little runner, Micky,' said Dad, ruffling his hair. 'It's nice to see you dashing about a bit and having fun.'

Micky glowed. He walked along beside Dad, skipping and hopping a bit to match Dad's long loping stride. He suddenly didn't feel like a baby any more. He didn't even feel like a boy. He felt like a man.

Then a werewolf sprang right out of the wooded garden and Micky shrieked.

'What the ...? For goodness' sake, Micky, it's

only a *corgi*!' Dad declared in disgust as Micky cowered away.

All right, it was only an old lady's corgi, although it was a belligerent one, barking its head off at poor Micky. It looked like a pint-sized werewolf on mini legs.

'Help,' wailed Micky.

'It's all right, dear, he won't hurt you,' said the old lady.

'Pull yourself together, Micky,' said Dad, giving him a shake. 'What's the matter with you?'

'Leave him, love,' said Mum, slipping her arm round Micky. 'He's just a bit scared of dogs at the moment, that's all.'

'I could understand it if it was a socking great Rottweiler, but a corgi!' said Dad.

He didn't say any more, but Micky felt he was in disgrace.

He tried to soothe himself after tea by doing another drawing of his magic land. Marigold came bustling up, but Mum found her some old white net curtains so she could play weddings with all her Little Ponies, and that kept her well out of Micky's way. She made a wedding frock for each Little Pony and married them all off to each other.

Dad pointed out that she'd got it wrong but Marigold didn't care.

'My ponies don't want to marry boy ponies. They don't like boys. They can't be bothered with them,' said Marigold.

Dad looked as if he might agree.

Micky drew and coloured carefully but the magic land wouldn't come right this time. He used the wrong purple for the mountains by mistake and so they looked dark and frightening. The lake looked cold and bleak. The meadows were bare and the woods were the worst. He tried to make them look real by crayoning in all the brown trunks under the wavy green leaf part. It didn't work. It just looked as if there were a lot of brown things in the wood. Brown creatures. Werewolves.

The werewolves even spoilt going to tea with Granny Boot on Sunday. Granny Boot was Micky's favourite person in all the world. Her name wasn't really Boot, it was just a nickname.

Micky had made it up for her. Granny Boot had a second-hand clothes shop and every Saturday and Sunday she got up very early and went to Car Boot Sales to get stock for her shop. She sometimes took Micky with her for a great treat. She said he had an eye for a bargain. The older girls weren't interested and Mona moaned and Marigold picked things up and dropped them, but Micky and Granny always had a very good time at the Boot Sales.

'You're my Granny Boot,' said Micky, giving her a hug.

Dad laughed and laughed when he heard Granny's new name.

'Yes, she's an Old Boot all right,' Dad chuckled, and Mum got cross.

After they'd all had a lovely tea at Granny's (ham salad sandwiches and jam sponge and chocolate finger biscuits and raspberry jelly and ice cream) she took Micky upstairs to show him the bargains she'd found at that morning's Boot Sale.

'Look at this lovely little fifties number with its sweetheart neckline,' said Granny, holding up a faded blue dance frock. 'You could do a lovely quickstep in this, all right.'

She danced round her bedroom in her fluffy slippers holding the frock in front of her, while Micky sat on her bed and laughed.

Then Granny Boot delved into her pile of newly bought clothes on the floor and found a

shrivelled swimming costume with funny
padded bits at the front.

'I don't think I'd even get one leg into this
skimpy little thing,' said Granny Boot. She tied it
on to her head instead, with the padded bits
sticking straight up as decoration.

Micky laughed so much he nearly fell off the
bed.

'Don't you laugh at my lovely new hat, you
cheeky monkey,' said Granny Boot. 'Now,
where's that old fox-fur cape, that'll set it off a
treat.'

She stirred the pile of old clothes – and a
ginger werewolf leapt out of their midst, eyes
beady, teeth bared.

Micky screamed.

'What's up, my little lovie?' said Granny Boot,
rushing to him – but she had hold of the fox-fur
cape, so the werewolf rushed too, and Micky
went on screaming until Mum came and worked
out what was worrying him.

Poor Granny Boot was very upset and shut the
fox-fur cape right away in her wardrobe.

'I didn't mean to frighten you, my pet. Silly
old Granny Boot,' she kept saying. 'It's all my
fault.'

'It's Micky's fault for being such a milk pudding,' said Dad. 'You've got to stop this nonsense, Micky, do you hear me? Acting scared of a tatty bit of fur!'

'Micky's a milk pudding!' Marigold yelled delightedly.

'You shouldn't call the poor kiddie nasty names,' said Granny Boot, glaring at Dad.

'He shouldn't be such a coward.'

'Cowardy cowardy custard!' sang Marigold.

'He's not a coward, he's a brave little lad! He puts up with a lot, the way you keep picking on him,' said Granny Boot.

'I think it's time to go home,' Mum said quickly. 'Come on, you lot. Get your things.'

'You give your Granny Boot a big kiss,' said Granny Boot to Micky.

'I'm sorry I was silly,' said Micky in a small sniffly voice.

He took even longer to go to sleep that night. The bedroom was so dark he pulled the curtains open so that he could see a little in the moonlight. That was a mistake. Micky saw the round white globe in the sky. It was a full moon. Everyone knows werewolves are at their very worst on the night of a full moon.

3 · · ·

Mum looked at the dark circles under Micky's eyes in the morning.

'We've got to sort this out, old Mick,' she said.

'Yes, Mum,' said Micky. He looked at her. 'How?'

'I'll think of something,' said Mum.

Micky hoped Mum might think of something pretty rapidly. He found it very hard to get past Sandy the Alsatian, even right on the other side of the road. He had to run like mad, gasping for breath. Marigold ran after him, yelling taunts.

'Micky's scared of a silly old dog. Micky's scared of Alsatians. Micky's scared of corgis. Micky's scared of a hearthrug. Micky's scared of a silly bit of fur. Micky's scared, scared, scared.'

'Shut up,' said Micky, but Marigold wouldn't shut up. She put up her hands like paws and went woof-woof-woof right in Micky's face.

Micky managed to escape her for lessons but she was there in the playground at break, with a whole hen-party of her horrible little friends.

Marigold put up her paws and did the woof-woof-woof trick. And then all the friends put up their paws and went woof-woof-woof too.

Micky went scarlet. She'd told them. He couldn't believe that even Marigold would be so hateful.

'Silly little idiots,' he said, trying to sound scornful, but then one of them crept up behind him and went woof right in his ear. Micky jumped and they all cackled with laughter.

He tried to give them the slip at lunchtime, sloping off by himself behind the bike-sheds. But Darren Smith and all his gang were behind the bike-sheds too, sharing the stub of a cigarette and telling dirty jokes. 'What do you want, Micky Mouse?' said Darren.

'Nothing,' said Micky quickly.

'You spying on us?'

'Of course not,' Micky gabbled. You didn't ever argue with Darren or any of his gang or you ended up embedded in the playground.

'Then clear off, Micky Mouse. Go on. Go and play with the girls, where you belong.'

'I can't stick girls,' said Micky, though he had started to back away respectfully.

'Micky! Micky! Woofy-woofy-woof!' Marigold

and her cackling cronies had spotted him and had him cornered.

'Oooh I say, Micky Mouse plays with the *baby* girls,' said Darren.

'I don't play with them,' said Micky, but they were determined to play with him.

They danced round him in a circle, barking fit to bust.

'What are they on about?' said Darren. 'Why are they barking?'

'Because they're barking mad, that's why,' Micky joked desperately.

If Marigold told Darren and his mates that Micky was scared of werewolves, dogs, and indeed anything vaguely furry with teeth, then Micky's life wouldn't be worth living. As Marigold very well knew. Her blue eyes shone triumphantly. She didn't tell Darren. She just shook her head and giggled. But Micky knew she *might* tell.

Micky worried about it all afternoon. He didn't pay any attention to his teacher, Miss Monk. This was most unusual, because he was secretly passionately in love with Miss Monk. She had long black hair that shone almost blue in the sunlight and she had a dimple in each cheek when she smiled. She generally smiled a lot and the children smiled back. Everyone liked Miss Monk – even Darren Smith and his gang, though they played her up a lot and called her Old Monkey Face behind her back.

Darren and Co were silly in maths, flicking ink bombs at each other and making rude noises. Miss Monk got cross. She also got cross with Micky because he was in such a dream he copied down all the wrong sums.

'That was a silly waste of time, wasn't it?' said Miss Monk.

'Yes, Miss,' Micky agreed, miserable that he'd irritated his Beloved.

The last lesson was Art, Micky's favourite. Miss Monk started giving out big pieces of sugar paper and boxes of coloured chalks. Micky leapt to help her, to make amends, but when he handed Darren his box, Darren deliberately dropped it on the floor.

'Oh, Micky, you are clumsy!' said Darren.

'Do be careful with those chalks, they break so easily,' said Miss Monk. 'Watch what you're doing, Micky.'

Micky slunk back to his seat. He was too upset to listen properly while Miss Monk told the

children to draw a picture of the moon. She talked a lot about the moon and what it might look like and she told them about the men who had landed there in their spaceship. All the children but Micky listened hard and drew little spacemen and the weird rocky surface of the moon, using the silver and grey and dark blue chalks.

Micky picked up his silver chalk too and drew a round moon at the top of his paper. A full moon. He picked up the brown chalk, his hand shaking. He drew a huge werewolf with an evil face and enormous bared fangs. Then he got the red chalk and drew a little pinman person sticking out of the werewolf's mouth, dripping a great deal of blood. His hand was shaking so badly that he couldn't draw properly at all, and his wet palm made horrible smears in the chalk.

'What on earth are you drawing, Micky?' said Miss Monk.

Micky clenched his damp smudgy fists and said nothing.

'I thought I told you to draw the moon?'

Micky pointed shakily at the silver ball at the top of the paper.

'So what's this horrible big brown creature?'

Micky swallowed. He couldn't say. They'd all laugh at him.

'Let's have a look,' said Darren, craning his neck. 'I thought you were supposed to be good at drawing, Micky Mouse. It looks like a great big monkey being sick. Hey! I know who it is. Micky's drawn Old Monkey Face!'

All the children but Micky giggled and spluttered and nudged each other.

'Be quiet, Darren. Calm down all of you,' said Miss Monk, her dimpled cheeks very pink. 'And as for you, Micky, you'd better stay behind after school and do me a proper picture of the moon. I don't know why you're being so silly today.'

Micky knew why but he couldn't explain. He stayed sitting at his desk when the bell went and all the other children ran out of the classroom.

'Now, Micky, I'm really cross with you,' said Miss Monk, starting to gather up the drawings from the desks.

Micky sniffed and bent his head.

'You're not usually so naughty.'

'I'm sorry, Miss,' Micky mumbled.

'Well. I suppose we all have our off days. You don't have to stay after school. You can do me a picture at home tonight instead. Run along now.'

Micky didn't run. He hovered, biting his lip.

'What is it, Micky?' said Miss Monk, sighing.

'Miss, do you believe in werewolves?'

'Do I believe in …? No,' said Miss Monk firmly, gathering more drawings.

Micky gathered too, helping her.

'You're absolutely sure there's no such thing? Not ever, not anywhere?'

Miss Monk gathered his own messy picture. She looked at it carefully.

'Ah,' she said. 'I see. A werewolf. And a full moon. I'm with you. You mustn't worry about werewolves, Micky. They really don't exist. I promise they don't.' But then she bent down beside him and whispered in his ear. 'Only I'll tell you a secret, Micky. I got this film from the video shop the other day. *Savage Snarl*. And it was so creepy that I *almost* started believing in werewolves myself.'

'Oh, Miss! I've seen that film too,' Micky breathed.

'I thought so. Well, we're a silly pair, aren't we? No more horror videos for either of us, OK?'

'OK, Miss Monk.'

Micky skipped out into the playground feeling much happier. But then he saw Mum in the Mini parked outside the school gate, with Marigold in the back.

'Come on, Micky, all the rest of your class came out ages ago,' Mum called.

'Woof-woof-woof,' said Marigold, scrabbling at him as he got in the car.

'You shut up,' Micky hissed. He frowned at his mother. 'Why have you got the car, Mum? Oh no, we're not going shopping, are we?'

'We're sort of shopping,' said Mum, driving off. 'We're going to get a pet.'

'A pet?' said Micky warily. He wasn't very keen on pet animals. Meryl had two grey rabbits called Rachel and Roberta. Roberta had

originally been christened Robert and Meryl
had hoped Rachel and Robert would produce
lots of Little Grey Rabbits. But Rachel and
Roberta lived in happy sisterly spinsterhood
instead.

Micky much preferred Rachel and Roberta to
Wilbur, Mandy's white rat. He had very beady
red eyes and a long pink tail like a worm, and
Micky didn't ever go near his cage beside
Mandy's bed. She once tried wearing him draped
over her shoulder when she walked down the
street, but she sent several old ladies into
screaming hysterics and Mum was furious.

Mona used to own a very fat guinea-pig called
Dandelion, but he keeled over in his cage one day
and Mona found him lying paws in the air. She

was very upset and wanted to give him a proper burial in a purple Cadbury's chocolate box coffin, but Dandelion was too fat to fit. They had to use a shoebox instead. Micky painted it with yellow and green dandelions to try to make it look decorative, but Mona wasn't particularly grateful.

'Are we getting another guinea-pig for Mona?' Micky asked.

'No. I think it's time we got a pet for you, Micky,' said Mum.

'And for me,' said Marigold. 'I want a pony, Mum. A real live pony, a white one with a long mane and tail so I can groom it and plait it and tie it with ribbons.'

'Don't be silly, Marigold. Where on earth could we keep a pony?' said Mum. 'No, it's Micky's turn just now.'

'I'm not sure I want it to be my turn,' said Micky. 'What's it going to be if it's not a guinea-pig? I definitely don't want a rat.'

'I could keep my pony in Dad's garden shed, easy-peasy,' said Marigold. 'A white pony, and I'll call him Sugar Lump. And I'll ride him bare back and teach him tricks and then we can perform together in a circus.'

'Yes, you could perform in a circus, all right,'

Micky muttered. 'The performing chimpanzee. Ouch!'

'Marigold! Stop hitting your brother,' said Mum.

'Well, he said . . .'

'Look, I don't care. Behave yourselves, both of you. Now, I think the dogs' home is down this next road.'

'The dogs' home?' said Micky, going white.

'The dogs' home?' said Marigold, and her blue eyes started to shine.

'I'm not having a dog,' said Micky.

'It would be a good idea,' said Mum. 'Just a little dog. A very friendly one. Maybe a puppy. We'll have to see what they've got.'

'No,' said Micky.

'Yes,' said Mum.

'No, no, no!' said Micky, but Mum just drove on.

She drew up outside a white house with a notice saying Webb's Dog Shelter. Micky hunched up in his seat, imagining hundreds of dogs sheltering behind those white walls. He pictured them grinding their teeth and sharpening their claws. Then Mum opened the car door and he heard a high-pitched *howl* . . .

4 · · ·

'Please, Mum,' Micky begged. 'I can't go in there!'

Mum wouldn't listen. She made Micky get out of the car.

She knocked on the front door of the dogs' home. The howling increased, and then there was a lot of barking too. Micky clung to Mum's arm, and even Marigold took a step backwards. The door opened and a young freckled woman in jeans stood there smiling, surrounded by two barking Labradors, the colour of clotted cream, and a small black Scottie who kept diving through the Labradors' legs.

'Quiet, you silly dogs,' the woman shouted. She saw Micky shrinking away and said quickly, 'It's OK, they're all very friendly. They won't bite. There's no need to be frightened of them.'

'*I'm* not frightened,' said Marigold, squatting down to pet the Scottie, while the two Labradors sniffed and nuzzled. 'Aren't they lovely? What are their names? Shall we have the little Scottie dog,

Mum? Although I like the big creamy dogs too. Oh look, this one's *smiling* at me.'

'That's Tumble. And that's her brother Rough.'

'Oh great. We're a sister and brother and we can *have* a sister dog and brother dog.'

'No, I'm afraid Rough and Tumble are my dogs. And wee Jeannie here. But there are plenty of other lovely dogs to choose from out the back. I've got lots of strays at the moment. Come through to the kennels.'

'I'll wait outside,' Micky hissed, trying to dodge Rough and Tumble's big wet licks.

'Don't be silly, Micky,' said Mum. 'This is going to be your dog. You've got to choose.'

'I'll choose for him,' said Marigold, still playing with Jeannie. She rolled over and let Marigold tickle her tummy. 'There, look! She loves being tickled, doesn't she? It's my magic trick of taming all dogs. Maybe I'll be a dog trainer in a circus as well as a bare-back rider.'

'I think it's a trick that only works with little friendly dogs like Jeannie,' said Miss Webb. 'You shouldn't even touch some of the big dogs I've got out the back, just in case.'

'I'm not scared of any dogs, even really big ones,' Marigold boasted. 'Not like my brother.

He's older than me too, and yet he's *ever* so scared.'

'No I'm not,' Micky said hoarsely, but at that moment Jeannie nudged against his leg and he gave a little yelp of terror.

'See that!' said Marigold triumphantly. 'He's even scared of a little Scottie. He's hopeless, isn't he? I don't know why Mum wants to get him a dog, it's just daft, isn't it? She ought to get me a dog, seeing as I'm the one that likes them. And dogs don't need a special stable, do they? Just a little kennel.'

'Or even an old cardboard box,' said Miss Webb. 'I've got special big kennels at the back of my house because I always have so many stray dogs on my hands.' She turned back to Micky. 'But it's OK, they're all in separate pens and they can't get out.'

'He'll still be scared,' said Marigold. 'He's even scared of me.' She suddenly darted at Micky, going woof-woof-woof and poor Micky was so strung up and startled by this time that he jumped and very nearly burst into tears.

'Marigold!' said Mum, but she gave Micky a shake too, obviously embarrassed.

Marigold just laughed and Miss Webb was

trying hard to keep a straight face. Micky blinked desperately, and tried to swallow the lump in his throat. His face was scarlet, his whole body burning.

'We've got some puppies out the back,' said Miss Webb. 'They're really sweet and cuddly. I'd have a puppy if I were you.'

Micky's throat ached so much he could barely speak.

'I don't really want any dog. Not even a puppy, thank you,' he croaked.

'Just take a look, Micky,' said Mum, giving him a little push.

So Micky had to go with them to the kennels at the back of the house. The howling got louder. It had a strange eerie edge to it. Marigold put her hands over her ears.

'Which one's making that horrid noise?' she complained.

'Yes, sorry. That's a stray we picked up last night. He's been making that row ever since, though we've done our best to comfort him. He's only a puppy, but he's a vicious little thing all the same. I certainly wouldn't recommend him for a family pet, especially as the little boy's so nervous.'

'I bet I could tame him,' Marigold boasted. She approached the pen in the corner, where a big grey puppy stood tensely, head back, howling horribly.

'Nice doggie,' said Marigold, and the puppy quivered and then stopped in mid-howl.

'See that!' said Marigold excitedly. 'There, I've stopped him. He's coming over to see me. Here, boy. You like me, don't you? Do you want to be my doggie, eh? You can't be Micky's dog because he's such a silly little wet wimp.'

Micky couldn't stand the word wimp. It sounded so horrible and feeble and ugly and pimply.

'Don't call Micky silly names,' said Mum.

'Well, it's true. He really is a wimp. Even Dad says so,' said Marigold, reaching through the bars to pat the strange grey puppy. 'Dad says I should have been his boy because I've got all the spark, while Micky's just a wimp.'

Micky burned all over. He shut his eyes, his whole skin prickling, itching unbearably. He could still hear the howling but now it seemed to be right inside his own head. He ground his teeth . . . and then suddenly Marigold screamed.

Micky opened his eyes. He stared at his shrieking sister. The grey puppy had a fierce grip of her finger and was biting hard with his little razor teeth.

'Get it off me! Help, help! Oh, Mum, help, it hurts!' Marigold yelled.

A very naughty little grin bared Micky's teeth – almost as if he was biting too. Then he shook his head and Marigold managed to snatch her finger away from the savage little pup.

'*Bad* boy,' said Miss Webb to the excited puppy. 'I'm so sorry he went for you, dear. Mind you, I did try to warn you. You mustn't ever take silly risks with stray dogs. Let's have a look at that finger and see what damage has been done.'

'It's bleeding!' Marigold screamed.

'Come on now, lovie, it's only a little scratch,' said Mum, giving her a cuddle.

'Still, it's better not to take any risks. We'll give it a dab of disinfectant and find you a bandage,' said Miss Webb.

She led the wailing Marigold back into the house. Mum followed, looking a little agitated.

Micky didn't follow. He stayed where he was, out by the dog pens. He took no notice of all the ordinary dogs obedient in their pens. He didn't even give the cute Labrador puppies snuggled in their basket a second glance. He only had eyes for the strange grey puppy that had bitten Marigold.

It ran towards Micky. Micky didn't back away. He didn't feel so scared. And the puppy seemed to have perked up too. He didn't howl any more. He made little friendly snuffling sounds.

'You just bit my sister,' Micky whispered.

The puppy coughed several times. It sounded almost as if he was chuckling. Micky started giggling too.

'That was bad,' Micky spluttered, his hand over his mouth so they wouldn't hear back in the house. 'But we don't care, do we?'

The puppy shook his head. He came right up

against the bars of his pen, sticking out his soft pointed snout. His amber eyes were wide and trusting now.

'Are you trying to make friends?' Micky asked.

The puppy snuffled.

'Hello, puppy,' Micky said, and he reached through the bars to pat the puppy's head, though Marigold had just demonstrated that this was a very dangerous thing to do.

'But you're not going to bite me, are you?' said Micky.

The puppy twitched his nose and blinked his eyes. Micky very gently touched the coarse grey fur. His hand was trembling. The puppy quivered too, but stayed still. Micky held his breath and started stroking very softly. The puppy pressed up even closer, in spite of the hard bars. His pink tongue came out and he licked Micky's bare knee.

'We're pals, right?' Micky whispered.

The puppy licked several times.

'Hey, I'm not a lollipop,' Micky giggled, wiping at his slobbery knee.

The puppy licked harder, sharing the joke. He managed to get one paw through the bars. He held it out to Micky. Micky shook the hard little pad solemnly.

'How do you do,' said Micky. 'I'm Micky. And that silly girl you bit was my sister Marigold.'

The puppy grinned wolfishly.

'You didn't half go for her, didn't you,' said Micky, and they had another giggle together, the puppy giving little barks of glee.

'Micky! Get away from that dog!' Mum suddenly cried, rushing out of the back of the house. 'How can you be so stupid? Look what he just did to Marigold.'

'He won't bite me,' said Micky calmly.

'Do as your mum says,' said Miss Webb, returning with Marigold. Marigold was still blotched with tears and she held her bandaged finger high in the air to show it off. 'That puppy is much too unpredictable. I don't know what I'm going to do with him.'

'I'll take him as my pet,' said Micky, and the puppy stiffened and then licked him rapturously.

'Don't be silly, Micky,' said Mum, trying to pull him away.

'I'm not being silly, Mum. I want this dog,' said Micky.

'No!' Marigold protested. 'We're not having that horrible mangy nasty thing. It bites. My finger hurts and hurts. I shall maybe have to go to the hospital to get it all stitched up.'

'Marigold, I told you, it's only a scratch,' said Mum. 'Now, Micky, leave that bad puppy alone and come and look at some of the other dogs.'

'No, Mum. I want this one. Please. I must have this puppy.'

'What about these other puppies over here? They're half Labradors and they're very gentle and docile. Look at the little black one with the big eyes. He'd make a much better pet. See, he's much prettier than that puppy there,' said Miss Webb.

'I don't mind him not being pretty. I like the

way he looks,' said Micky, and he had both arms through the bars now, holding the puppy tight.

'Micky, will you leave go of him?' said Mum. 'You're really the weirdest little boy. One minute you're scared stiff of all dogs and then the next you make friends with the most vicious little creature. What is it, anyway? Alsatian?'

'It's certainly mostly German Shepherd but it's got something else mixed up with it. Something very odd,' said Miss Webb.

'I know,' said Micky, nodding solemnly. 'And I want him so. Oh, Mum, please, please, please.'

'No, he's not to have him, Mum! He'll bite me again,' Marigold protested furiously.

Mum dithered between the two of them, looking helpless. Micky looked up at her, his big brown eyes glinting amber in the sunlight.

'You said it was going to be my pet. I had to choose him. And I've chosen,' said Micky.

Mum sighed. 'All right, then. You can have that one if you really must. Only I still think it's a very silly choice.'

Micky knew it was the only possible choice. He had the most magical special pet in the whole world. His very own werewolf. Well, not quite a werewolf yet. A werepuppy.

5

'What are you going to call your puppy?' said Mum, starting up the car.

'I'm not sure,' said Micky, pondering. The werewolf in *Savage Snarl* hadn't really had a name. Maybe Mandy would hire it from the video shop again when Mum and Dad weren't around. The werepuppy would like to watch one of its relations. Micky was sure he wouldn't be scared this time, not if he had his own werepuppy on his lap. He didn't need to be scared of werewolves any more (and that included any ordinary dopey old dogs). He'd been specially chosen by the werepuppy. It looked up to him. Micky was the Leader of the Were-Pack.

'I think he should call it the Raving Slavering Savage Monster,' said Marigold, nursing her sore finger. 'You're mad letting him have that horrid ugly beast, Mum.'

The werepuppy stiffened on Micky's lap. He started fidgeting.

'Sh, boy. It's OK. I'm here,' said Micky, stroking

him. He glared at Marigold. 'Don't you dare call my puppy names. He's not a bit ugly. He's beautiful.'

'He's hideous. Just like you,' said Marigold, pulling a face at both of them. 'My brother's dog belongs down the bog.' She cackled with laughter. 'Hey, did you hear that? My brother's dog ...'

'That's enough, Marigold,' said Mum wearily.

The werepuppy fidgeted some more, so that Micky had difficulty hanging on to him.

'What's the matter, boy?' Micky said softly.

The werepuppy started to howl.

'Oh no! Hark at it,' said Marigold, covering her ears.

'I don't think he likes the car,' said Micky.

The werepuppy howled harder.

'Yes, it makes him feel sick,' said Micky.

'You make *me* feel sick,' said Marigold. 'My brother Micky makes me sicky. My brother Micky ...'

'Marigold!' said Mum.

'... makes me sicky,' Marigold whispered.

The werepuppy gave one last howl, wrenched himself free from Micky's embrace, bounded on to Marigold, and was very sick indeed all down her front and into her lap.

Mum had to stop the car and attempt a grand mopping-up operation. Marigold screamed non-stop while this was going on. Micky took the werepuppy for a little walk in the fresh air. He seemed much better now. He grinned wolfishly up at Micky. Micky grinned back.

'Naughty old Wolfie,' he said, giving him a pat.

The werepuppy gave his little cough that sounded exactly like a chuckle.

'Yep, that's what I'm going to call you. Wolfie,' said Micky.

He introduced Wolfie to Meryl, Mandy and Mona at home while Mum and Marigold were upstairs in the bathroom.

'Yuck! Whatever made you choose that ugly old thing?' said Mona.

Wolfie bared his teeth indignantly and snarled.

'Help! He's savage too,' said Mona, backing nervously.

'Yes. He's already bitten Marigold. So you'd better watch out,' said Micky.

'You're going to have to train him properly,' said Meryl bossily. 'I'll help you, if you like. He's got to learn about meal times and going to the loo and —'

Wolfie did a little puddle there and then, right in the middle of the living-room carpet.

'Um, look!' said Mona.

'Stop him, Micky,' said Meryl, going pink.

'It's your fault,' said Micky. 'You told him to go to the loo so he did.'

'Take him out to the garden,' said Mandy. 'And then you'd better get that puddle mopped up before Mum sees.'

Mum came running down the stairs that moment and saw all right.

'One mess after another,' she said crossly, fetching a bucket and mop. 'Marigold's right, you know. I must be mad.'

'You're not a bit mad, Mum. You're the loveliest mother in all the world for getting me Wolfie,' said Micky.

He caught hold of Mum and hugged her, and Wolfie joined in enthusiastically too, licking Mum's legs.

'You get that naughty puppy away from me,' said Mum. 'Find him a little patch in the garden where he can go when he needs to.'

'Come on then, Wolfie,' said Micky, and they trotted off together.

Wolfie liked the garden a lot. He raced up and

down the grass. He also raced up and down the flower beds.

'Hey, Wolfie! Not on that bit! Oh, Dad's flowers. Here, boy. Bad boy! No!'

Wolfie laughed and lolloped along, clearly saying yes.

'What's Dad going to say?' said Micky, looking at the flattened flowers.

Wolfie grinned, showing all his teeth. Werepuppies obviously didn't worry about dads. Micky couldn't feel too worried himself because he was having so much fun.

Wolfie suddenly sniffed and stiffened.

'What is it? Are you feeling sick again, Wolfie?' Micky asked.

Wolfie was feeling anything but sick. His yellow eyes were narrowed on the little hutch at the end of the garden. Wolfie smacked his chops, slavering a little.

'What is it, Wolfie? That's just Rachel and Roberta, Meryl's pet rabbits.'

Wolfie didn't seem to think they were pets. He was looking at them as if they were a very tasty lunch. He stalked slowly towards the hutch, dribbling.

'*No,* Wolfie. Bad boy,' said Micky, checking on

the little catch at the side of the hutch.

Rachel and Roberta quivered inside, their pink noses twitching in distress.

'It's all right, girls. I'll protect you. I won't let him get you,' said Micky in a lordly way.

Wolfie was pawing at the rabbit hutch, his little claws right on the catch. It wouldn't take him long to find out how to undo it.

'*No!*' said Micky, but Wolfie didn't seem to be taking much notice.

Micky needed to get the rabbits right out of harm's way, somewhere high up where Wolfie couldn't reach them. Micky looked round the garden. He looked at the garden shed. He looked at the flat top of the garden shed. Then he scooped the struggling Wolfie under his arm and somehow or other got him into the garden shed.

'I'm going to have to tie you up in here, just for a minute or two, Wolfie, that's all,' said Micky.

Wolfie refused to understand. He got very upset indeed when Micky tried to tether him by one leg.

'It's just for a *minute*, Wolfie,' said Micky.

Wolfie behaved as if a minute might be an entire lifetime. He growled and howled and when Micky tried to pat him to reassure him he snapped at his hand, nearly biting him.

'Oh no you don't,' said Micky firmly. 'You're not to bite me. I'm your friend. We're pals, you and me. So you've got to learn to do as I say, right?'

Wolfie sniffed and grumbled, but he lowered his head submissively, and this time when Micky patted him he didn't snap at all.

'Wow,' said Micky softly. Wolfie really had done as he was told. No one had ever obeyed Micky before. He obviously couldn't tell Mum and Dad what to do. Meryl and Mandy and Mona would squash him if he tried to give them orders. Marigold always argued as a matter of course and did her best to boss him about instead.

'But we can boss her now, can't we, Wolfie?' said Micky. 'Right, you stay there, out of harm's way. I promise you, I'll just be two ticks.'

Micky took the stepladder and dragged it outside. He got a stout cardboard box to be temporary accommodation for the rabbits while he was fixing them up a desirable new residence. He leant the ladder against the wall of the garden shed. He undid the catch of the hutch and put first one then the other rabbit into the cardboard box. They were still in a shaky way, especially as Wolfie had started howling miserably inside the shed.

Then Micky took hold of the hutch and lifted it. It was quite a struggle. It was almost impossible holding it under one arm and trying to climb the ladder. He knew he ought to call one or other of his sisters to help him. Someone at least ought to hold on to the ladder in case it slipped. Micky had always hated ladders. When he was little Dad had taken him to the playground in the park and put him on the big ladder to go on the slide. Micky had got halfway up the ladder, and then looked down. That had been a mistake. He'd shut his eyes and screamed. Dad had had to climb up the ladder to rescue him. Dad hadn't been best pleased.

Micky shut his eyes momentarily, hating the memory.

Wolfie howled harder inside the shed. There was a sudden crash. Several further crashes, and frenzied barking. Wolfie had obviously got free. Micky had shut the door so Wolfie couldn't get out. He could, however, make quite a mess inside the shed. There was another bump and crash. Micky thought of all Dad's gardening things and the seed trays and the potted plants. Oh dear.

The rabbits were getting restless too. Micky could see Rachel's paws right at the top of the cardboard box. She was so fat she'd tip it right over any minute.

'Get cracking,' said Micky, and he quickly clawed his way up the ladder, hanging on grimly to the hutch as he climbed. It dug hard into the soft flesh of his arm, scratching and tearing, but it couldn't be helped. His whole shoulder felt dislocated as he struggled to keep hold of the hutch, and his hands were so slippy with sweat that he very nearly dropped it, he very nearly slipped himself, he very nearly stumbled right off the rung into thin air ... but he didn't! He got there. He got right to the top of the garden shed and he rolled the hutch on to it and then stood panting at the top of the ladder, stretching his freed arms in delight.

But he couldn't hang about. He hurried down the ladder, he picked up Rachel rabbit, tucking her right inside his T-shirt. He'd never been all that keen on rabbits and she scrabbled in a rather disgusting way, but it couldn't be helped. He climbed up the ladder, his T-shirt wriggling violently, he got the hutch door open, he deposited Rachel inside, he shut the catch, he scrambled down the ladder, he picked up Roberta, he posted her down his T-shirt too, he climbed up the ladder, he had a terrible job getting the hutch door open, keeping Rachel in while still struggling to extract Roberta from inside his shirt; he struggled and they wriggled and he swore at them and told them they were so silly they almost deserved to be turned into rabbit stew, but at long last Roberta was in the hutch with Rachel and the catch was closed on them both. He'd done it! The rabbits were safe, out of Wolfie's way, in a lovely new high-rise site.

'Yippy!' said Micky, and he practically bounced down the ladder. He got the garden shed door open and Wolfie flew at him, covered with earth and seedlings, barking joyously.

'What's that creature doing in my garden?'

It was Dad home from work. Micky quivered like the rabbits, his nostrils twitching. He looked at the fumbled flowers, the squashed shrubs, the earthquake spilling out of the garden shed. Dad seemed to be getting taller and fiercer and redder in the face, while Micky whizzed right down to a small scared mouse.

'This is my puppy, Dad,' Micky squeaked.

'Who said you could have a dog? I thought you were scared of them? Look at all this mess! You obviously haven't got a clue how to look after him. I'm not having this. You can't keep him.'

'But he's mine!' said Micky.

Wolfie barked to show that Micky was his.

'Look, you don't know anything about dogs. You can't let them run wild like this. You've got to let them know who's boss,' Dad shouted, showing Micky who was Boss.

Wolfie didn't like Dad's tone. He approached Dad with his teeth bared, growling.

'Don't you growl at me, you silly little puppy,' said Dad, and he put out a finger in warning.

This was a mistake. 'Ouch!' Dad yelled.

Wolfie bristled and growled, ready to have another go.

'Get away, you little brute. Quiet! Get off!' Dad cried.

Wolfie advanced rapidly. Dad started to back. He waved his hands about. He started sweating. He looked worried.

'Down, Wolfie!' Micky called. 'Here, boy. Come to me. It's OK, Dad. He won't really hurt you.'

And Wolfie shook his head and stopped growling, bounding over to Micky.

'That's my dad, Wolfie. You mustn't bite him, you bad boy,' said Micky, bending down and rubbing noses with Wolfie.

'Well I'm blowed,' said Dad, weakly.

'I'm ever so sorry about all the mess, Dad. I'll pay for some more flowers and seeds and stuff out of my pocket money, I promise.'

'He's turned the whole garden into a tip,' said Dad, but he didn't sound so cross now. 'And what on earth is that rabbit hutch doing on top of the shed?'

'Oh. Well, I had to put it there. Out of Wolfie's way,' said Micky.

'*You* put it there? You went up that ladder?'

'Yes, and I suppose it's going to be a bit of a nuisance for Meryl when she has to climb up to give Rachel and Roberta their supper, but I'll try to get Wolfie trained really soon. Only do let me keep him, Dad. I have to have him. It's like he's part of me already,' said Micky.

'I didn't know you had it in you, son,' Dad murmured. 'All right then, Micky. You can keep your puppy. For the moment.'

6 ...

It seemed a good idea to feed Wolfie as soon as possible as he'd already chewed several fingers, tried to eat a rabbit supper, and now, after a sniff at Wilbur rat and a gnaw at Mona, he was severely worrying Marigold's My Little Ponies.

'I'll get some proper dog food tomorrow,' said Mum. 'Meanwhile, I wonder if he'd like a hamburger? He certainly looks ready for proper meat. He's not a little baby puppy, he's more a boy.'

'Like me,' said Micky, helping Mum delve in the deep freeze. He found some frozen hamburgers and took one out of the packet. He held it up to Wolfie.

'Do you think you'd like this, Wolfie?'

Wolfie nodded enthusiastically. He leapt up and snatched the frozen hamburger right out of Micky's hand. He did his best to chomp it up, but his teeth skidded across the icy surface.

'You can't eat it like that, silly,' said Micky. 'You've got to wait until it thaws.'

Wolfie didn't want to wait. He gnawed and slobbered and licked the hamburger like an ice lolly. Micky knew that ordinary wolves came from the North so maybe Wolfie had a built-in love of frozen food.

He seemed to have a built-in love of any food whatsoever. Wolfie wanted more than his share of the hamburgers when they were cooked — *and* most of Micky's chips and peas. He noisily demanded a big lick of ice cream afterwards, though Mum got very cross and wouldn't let him share Micky's bowl. Wolfie particularly wanted a chocolate biscuit when they had a cup of tea. Micky showed him how to sit up and beg and Wolfie got the hang of it immediately.

He scurried round to Mandy and begged appealingly, and she laughed and gave him half of her biscuit.

'He's not getting any of *my* biscuit,' said Marigold, stuffing it into her mouth so quickly she choked. 'Horrid ugly old thing, keep it away from me!' she coughed, spraying biscuit crumbs everywhere.

'Not Marigold, Wolfie. We wouldn't want her messy soggy old biscuit anyway,' said Micky.

Wolfie steered well clear of Marigold and

edged up to Meryl, who had only taken one bite of her biscuit so far.

'Beg for it, then, Wolfie,' said Micky.

Wolfie sat up and begged.

'See, Meryl, he's trained already,' Micky boasted.

He spoke a little too soon. As soon as Wolfie devoured Meryl's biscuit he stood up, circled the room in a purposeful way, and then squatted.

'Oh no!' Mum wailed. 'Not again!'

'Worse!' said Mandy, giggling.

'*Yuck!*' said Mona.

'Show him what he's done and then take him out in the garden, son,' said Dad.

Micky did his best. Wolfie didn't seem at all ashamed. He didn't want to leave the room, especially when there were still chocolate biscuits on offer. He argued with Micky, snapping at him.

'Watch out, Micky,' said Mum.

'It's OK. He won't really hurt me. Come on, you messy old pup. Out, I say,' said Micky sternly, and Wolfie slunk to his side.

'I'd never have thought it of him,' Dad muttered. 'Our Micky's got so much spirit when he wants. And that pup's got an evil temper. He went for me, and I don't mind admitting, I wasn't too thrilled about it – but Micky seems quite fearless.'

Micky swaggered out into the garden with Wolfie. He found a spare patch of earth (there were quite a few, actually, after Wolfie's race across the flower patch) and tried to explain to Wolfie that this was now his own special toilet. Wolfie found the whole thing a huge joke and dashed about grinning, refusing to listen properly.

He disgraced himself again before bedtime. The whole house was starting to reek of disinfectant and Mum was thoroughly regretting Wolfie's adoption.

'I've a good mind to take him straight back to the dogs' home tomorrow,' she said grimly, still scrubbing at the carpet.

'Mum!' said Micky.

'It's OK, son, Mum doesn't mean it,' said Dad. 'She's just a bit narked because of her poor carpet. I don't think that pup's going to make it out into the garden for a bit. We'd better put newspaper down. Then the minute he starts to tiddle – or worse – we'll pop him on the newspaper. He'll soon get the hang of it.'

'Thanks, Dad,' said Micky. He was kneeling on the carpet, one arm round Wolfie, the other busily crayoning a new moon picture for Miss Monk. He was trying hard now, using his best cartridge paper and his biggest set of felt-tips. He coloured the vast rocky surface of the moon and a strange purple sky and a little tiny blue and green earth spinning so far away. He did a rocket on the moon, and tumbling out of it, taking their first joyous leaps into the moon's atmosphere, were two tiny silver figures in spacesuits. One was upright, the other on all fours.

Marigold stopped grooming her panicky ponies back into submission and walked past, kicking out with her feet as she went, sort of accidentally on purpose. But just as her slipper touched Micky's drawing hand, Wolfie growled ferociously and Marigold jumped smartly out of the way.

Wolfie himself wasn't so sensible. He was so keen to see Micky's picture that he slavered admiringly and made a long slimy smudge all down one side, and then he struggled free of Micky's restraining arm at one point and pranced right across the paper, leaving several muddy paw prints.

'Wolfie, you nuisance!' said Micky. He usually found it unbearable when his pictures got spoiled, and this was one of his best efforts. He had to show it to Miss Monk too, and she might not understand this time. But somehow Micky didn't feel too worried.

'Time for bed, Micky and Marigold,' said Mum. 'Now, what about Wolfie? Where's he going to sleep?'

'Locked up in the garden shed,' said Marigold.

'My rabbits don't want him howling underneath them. They're unsettled enough as it is. Rabbits are supposed to live in burrows, not blooming great skyscrapers,' said Meryl.

'If Wolfie's got to sleep in the garden shed then I'm sleeping with him,' said Micky.

'You're scared of the dark, Sicky-Micky,' said Marigold.

'I wouldn't be scared, not with Wolfie,' said Micky, and Wolfie growled in agreement.

'No one's sleeping outside,' said Mum.

'Then Wolfie can come and sleep with me,' Micky said excitedly.

'You're not having that puppy in your bed. I absolutely forbid it,' Mum said firmly. 'I think we'll try bedding Wolfie down in a corner of the kitchen. Later on we'll get him a proper basket but for now we'd better make do with a cardboard box. Marigold, where's that big box I gave you when we came back from Sainsbury's?'

'You can't have that! It's My Little Ponies special stable extension,' said Marigold indignantly.

'We'll get you another box tomorrow, a better one. But Wolfie needs it for tonight,' said Mum, and for once Marigold couldn't talk her out of it.

Wolfie didn't seem particularly grateful. Mum found him an old blanket and made him up a very comfortable bed inside the box and Micky settled him into it with a biscuit to nibble on, but Wolfie bounded up again as soon as he'd demolished the biscuit. Micky said goodnight firmly and shut the door on him. Wolfie howled reproachfully and scrabbled at the kitchen door. He went on howling and scrabbling most of the evening. Mona and Mandy and Meryl went to bed. Wolfie didn't go to bed. He howled and scrabbled. Mum and Dad went to bed. Wolfie still didn't go to bed. He howled and scrabbled, scrabbled and howled.

Micky couldn't stand it any longer. It wasn't poor Wolfie's fault. Werewolves were nocturnal. Wolfie couldn't be expected to go to sleep. And he sounded so lonely howling away all by himself in the kitchen. It was a dark night too. Wolfie was only a baby werewolf. Maybe he was a bit scared of the dark.

Micky was rather scared of the dark himself. Marigold was right on that account. He normally didn't like getting up in the night, not even to whizz along to the toilet and back. He certainly didn't want to go all the way downstairs. The stairs were the darkest part of the house, and they creaked at every step. He was always frightened hands might reach right through the banisters and grab his ankles. But now he was so worried about poor Wolfie that he jumped out of bed, shuffled across the landing in his slippers, and ran down the stairs determinedly. He decided that if there *were* any hands then he'd simply stamp on them.

He reached the downstairs hall perfectly safely. Wolfie's howl was becoming deafening. Micky opened the kitchen door and Wolfie flew at him, practically jumping into his arms. He licked Micky's face ecstatically, as if they'd been parted for several weeks instead of several hours.

'Silly old boy,' said Micky, giving Wolfie a big hug and lots of kisses. 'Come on. You've got to *try* to go to sleep. I'll put you back to bed in your box and then I'll stay and chat with you for a bit, OK?'

Micky felt his way uncertainly across the pitch black kitchen, Wolfie struggling in his arms. He wondered if he might be dreaming for a moment, because the kitchen floor seemed to have changed into a beach. His slippers crunched on a lot of gritty stuff like sand – and then he seemed to have reached the sea, because his slippers were soaked and he was almost paddling.

The moon suddenly came out from behind the thick clouds and Micky saw the kitchen properly. He stiffened with shock.

'Oh, Wolfie!' he gasped.

Bags of sugar were spread all over the floor, while chewed cartons of milk made a lake of the lino.

'You bad bad boy,' said Micky, and he gave Wolfie a little shake.

Wolfie gave a high-pitched howl and jumped right out of Micky's arms. He seemed a strange eerie silver in the moonlight, and yet his eyes glinted gold. He threw back his head and howled again, every inch a werewolf.

'Oh gosh,' said Micky, his skin prickling. 'Calm down now, Wolfie. Try to be a good little pup.'

The moonlight was making Wolfie want to be very bad indeed. He streaked round the room, slavering, his teeth gleaming. He'd had his very large meal of hamburgers and biscuits just a few hours ago but now he looked ravenously hungry.

Next door's tabby cat leapt up on to the outside window ledge on one of her nightly prowls. She saw Wolfie and her nose bumped the window pane in astonishment. Wolfie saw the tabby cat and dribbled ferociously, his teeth bared.

'Shoo!' Micky shouted, flapping his hand at the cat.

She didn't need to be told twice. She gave one yowl of terror and fled as Wolfie sprang. Micky leapt after him, catching him by one back paw. Wolfie's head banged hard against the window. Micky's head banged even harder against the wall. They ended up in a heap on the very sticky floor. They both moaned and grumbled at each other.

'You can't go round chomping up all the neighbourhood cats, Wolfie,' said Micky sternly. 'It's no use whining and telling me you're hungry. Here, why don't you lick up all this sugar?'

Wolfie wasn't interested in feeble food like sugar now. He wanted furry flesh.

'You've got to *try* to be a good boy,' said Micky, but Wolfie enjoyed being bad too much.

He struggled to his paws and shook his sore head, still salivating.

'Come back here,' said Micky, scrambling after him, but his feet skidded in the pool of milk and he fell headlong.

Wolfie went scampering across the kitchen and straight out the door.

'Come back!' Micky shouted, picking himself up and starting to run.

Wolfie stayed. There was a sudden savage growl and a heavy thud as Wolfie pounced on something.

'Oh goodness,' said Micky, charging into the living room.

Wolfie was violently attacking a large sheep,

going straight for its throat. He growled excitedly
but the sheep didn't even emit one baa. Micky
blinked and realized it was only the furry
hearthrug. He breathed a shuddering sigh of
relief – and then gasped again as Wolfie ripped
the rug into ribbons.

'No! Stop it, you awful animal! That's Mum's
and she'll be so cross. She'll send you back to that
shelter, you silly dog. Oh please, Wolfie, do try to
see sense.'

The moon suddenly went behind the clouds
again. Wolfie couldn't see anything, let alone
sense. He coughed in a confused manner. Micky
felt his way to the wall and switched on the light.

The hearthrug was in shreds. Wolfie whimpered amongst the strands of wool, furry balls caught in his sharp little claws. His fur was dark grey again, although covered in a positive cardi of white wool. His eyes had lost their golden glint. They were a clear amber and they clouded with fear as Micky marched up to him.

'Yes, you've been very very bad,' said Micky. 'But don't look so worried. I know you couldn't help it. Not really, anyway. But you're going to have to learn somehow or other. Now, how about helping me clear up some of this mess, eh?'

Wolfie trotted about as helpfully as he could, but he simply trod milk and sugar all over the carpet and spread the woolly balls back into the kitchen. Micky wasn't much more successful either, though he did as much mopping and sweeping as he could. He was tired out by the time he'd finished trying to set the rooms to rights.

'It's bedtime now. You in your bed here. Me in mine upstairs,' said Micky.

Wolfie shook his head determinedly. He leant against Micky, whimpering winningly.

'You can't come upstairs with me. Mum's

going to kill me as it is,' said Micky. 'So it looks
as if I'll have to snuggle up somehow with you,
Wolfie, doesn't it?'

Micky climbed resolutely inside the cardboard
box, hunching up on the blanket, his knees
digging into his chin. Wolfie jumped in readily
enough, panting happily.

'Don't breathe right in my face, Wolfie, it
tickles,' said Micky.

Wolfie licked instead.

'Old slobbery! Now come on, we've got to go
to sleep,' said Micky, glancing up at the window,
hoping the moon stayed well hidden. He put his
arms firmly round Wolfie and they both shut
their eyes and went to sleep at last.

7

They were woken by Mum's screams in the living room when she came downstairs in the morning and saw the shredded state of her hearthrug.

Micky crawled out of the cardboard box. Wolfie bounced out, not in the least concerned.

'*Micky!*' Mum shrieked.

'We're in here, Mum,' Micky mumbled.

Mum came rushing into the kitchen. She pulled up short when she saw the state it was in. She went as white as the spilled milk.

'I'm dreaming,' she croaked. 'Please let me be dreaming. First my lovely hearthrug —'

'Perhaps we could sew it together again?' Micky suggested in a small voice.

'Ha! And now look at this chaos! Tell me this is all a terrible nightmare and any minute I'm going to wake up and find we never took that wicked grey mutt into our house. Take him out of my sight, Micky, before I lose all control and shove him in a saucepan and serve scrambled dog for breakfast.'

'Yes, Mum. Sorry, Mum. And Wolfie's sorry too,' said Micky, trying to grab hold of him.

'Oh yes, he looks sorry, doesn't he? He's running around with a great grin on his face,' said Mum. 'Micky? Why are you all bent over? What's happened to your back and your legs? Micky, I think I'd better call the doctor.' Mum's voice was starting to get shrill.

'It's OK, Mum. I'm just a bit stiff. I spent the night curled up with Wolfie, you see.'

'I *told* you not to take him into your bed!' Mum shouted, her concern congealing.

'I didn't!' said Micky indignantly, lumbering about. 'I slept in Wolfie's bed. You didn't ever forbid me to do that. So it seemed like a good idea. At the time.'

'Oh, Micky. You silly little boy. You slept the entire night in a cardboard box?' said Mum.

'Well, some of the time I was awake.'

'Micky! Go and have a hot bath this minute. That'll ease some of the stiffness. And you'd better bath that bad puppy too, look at him, he's rolling in the milk! Go on, both of you. Shoo!'

The bent-over boy and the milkshake puppy disappeared. They returned in half an hour, upright and thoroughly scrubbed, surrounded by several aggravated sisters.

'Mum, it's not fair, it was *my* turn in the bathroom and Micky hogged it, and then when they came out at last Meryl jumped in front of me!'

'And I wish I hadn't because there were foul grey dog hairs all over the bath. Mum, he mustn't ever take that puppy in the bath like that, it's positively disgusting and we'll probably all end up with rabies.'

'I think I've got rabies already. My bite's still ever so sore. I think that stupid puppy should be put to sleep.'

'I wish he'd slept a bit last night. All that scrabbling and howling! Couldn't you shut him up, Micky?'

'You can all shut up for the moment and eat some breakfast,' said Mum. 'Come on, you're all going to be late for school.'

Dad was rushing round too, in his suit and his socks. He was holding one shoe in his hand and he looked distracted.

'Why don't you put your shoes on, dear?' said Mum.

'How can I put my wretched shoes on when

that daft dog's chewed this one to a pulp?' Dad shouted. 'What are you playing at, Micky? I thought you could keep him under control?'

'Sorry, Dad. I think he's teething.'

'Well, I hope he's not getting any *more* teeth,' said Dad. 'Where is he now?'

'Um. He was here just a minute ago,' said Micky.

'You've got to keep your eye on him!' said Dad.

Micky heard a proud little woof out in the hall. He ran to investigate. The morning paper was on the doormat. And Wolfie had performed right on top of it.

'My paper!' Dad bellowed.

'Well, you told him what to do, Dad. He's only trying to do as he's told. He's not to know it's the newspaper that you haven't read yet,' said Micky.

'Don't you take that tone of voice with me, Mr Smarty-Pants,' said Dad, and he brandished the chewed shoe as if he was going to use it to spank Micky.

Wolfie growled. Micky caught his breath. But then he looked Dad straight in the eyes and saw he wasn't being serious. Micky laughed, a little too loudly. Wolfie barked. And Dad gave them both a pat on the head and went off to work in his chewed shoe, minus his newspaper.

Meryl and Mandy and Mona went to school, some of them still unwashed. And Mum took Micky and Marigold to school.

'But what about Wolfie?' Micky said. 'Oh, Mum, I don't think I can go to school. Not just yet. Not till Wolfie's a bit bigger.'

'Don't be silly, Micky. I'll look after him for you.'

'Actually, Mum, I don't feel very well. I still feel stiff. Ever so. I don't think I'll be able to put my head up to see the blackboard. Maybe I'd better stay home just for today,' said Micky, contorting himself into a weird hunch.

'Micky! Stop playing up. Run into school now. Don't forget your moon picture for Miss Monk.'

Micky gave Wolfie many passionate hugs and kisses. Wolfie nuzzled him pathetically, whimpering.

'Oh, Mum! I can't go. Wolfie *needs* me!'

Micky found that he needed Wolfie too. He felt so little and lost without him. He kept reaching out for Wolfie and then finding he was patting thin air. Darren and his gang were at

school early, swaggering about the playground. Micky dodged behind a clump of little kids, but they spotted him.

'Ooh, what's that Micky Mouse has got in his lily-white little hand?' Darren shouted. 'A pretty picture for Old Monkey Face, eh?'

'Miss Monk,' said Micky. He hated that stupid nickname. Miss Monk had a positively beautiful face anyway.

'Ooooh, it's Miss Monk, is it,' said Darren, imitating Micky's voice, making him sound niminy piminy and prim.

'You shut up,' said Micky, in a very small voice.

Darren burst out laughing. He swaggered up

to Micky, curled his fingers up, and flicked his finger hard against Micky's nose.

'You going to make me shut up, eh?' said Darren.

Micky blinked. His nose stung badly. He hoped his eyes weren't going to water.

Darren's gang were all circling round, flicking at him too. Someone's hard finger prodded his back. Someone's nail scratched his neck. Micky whirled round, ducking and dodging. Darren snatched his picture from his flailing hand.

'What a load of rubbish,' he said, and he rolled the picture up into a tube and hit Micky on the head with it.

Micky gave a little squeak. Darren and his gang laughed. One of them gave him a push. Then another. Micky staggered a bit. It looked as if there might be a fight. And Micky certainly wasn't going to win.

'What are you boys up to?'

It was Miss Monk, scurrying across the playground, her long black hair bobbing about her shoulders, the folds of her flowery blue skirt flying out.

'Nothing, Miss,' said Darren quickly.

'What's going on, Micky?' said Miss Monk.

'Nothing, Miss,' said Micky too. He wasn't daft enough to tell tales, or Darren and his gang would tear his head off his shoulders after school.

'It looked like Something to me, not Nothing,' said Miss Monk. She reached for the rolled-up picture, and swiftly tapped Darren on the head with it.

'Silly little boy,' she said scathingly.

Darren went red, and some of the children in the playground nudged each other and giggled.

'Now go and stand in line. The bell's going to go any minute,' said Miss Monk. She unrolled the picture, and stood looking at it.

'We'll get you for this,' Darren whispered to Micky, and then he ran off with his gang.

Micky's stomach squeezed into a tight little ball. It wasn't fair. He hadn't told on them. What were they going to do to him? Oh help.

'This is a wonderful picture, Micky,' said Miss Monk, smiling at him.

Micky smiled back tentatively, almost forgetting about Darren.

'It got a bit mucked up, Miss,' he said.

'Well, I think it looks lovely. I particularly like the moon craters,' said Miss Monk, and she

pointed to the paw prints. 'And this shading is very effective to show the uneven surface.'

'It's more slurp than shading, Miss,' said Micky.

'A slurp?' said Miss Monk, laughing. 'So who was licking your picture, Micky? Your little sister Marigold?'

'No, Miss,' said Micky, giggling. 'No, it's my new puppy, Wolfie.'

'You've got a puppy! Oh, that's lovely for you. I am glad. You've called him Wolfie? That sounds a bit savage! He's not a baby werewolf, is he?'

'Well . . .' said Micky.

Miss Monk mistook his hesitation.

'Micky, you do know there's really no such thing as werewolves, don't you?'

'I'm not so sure, Miss,' said Micky.

'I know I said the other day that I was a bit frightened of werewolves – but I was really just joking,' said Miss Monk.

'Oh, I know, Miss. It's OK. I'm not a bit frightened of werewolves now,' said Micky, smiling up at her.

Then the bell rang and they had to go into school. Miss Monk pinned Micky's picture up on the wall, which pleased Micky a lot. Lessons weren't too bad either, and Micky might have relaxed and enjoyed himself if it hadn't been for Darren and his gang. They kept giving him meaningful glares. Micky started to dread the thought of lunchtime, when they might Get Him.

He scooted out ahead of the others and tried lurking by the steps, where the girls played. Marigold and her awful little friends were there, galloping up and down the steps pretending to be My Little Ponies, prancing and tossing their manes and pointing their hooves, but even their company was preferable to Darren and his gang.

Marigold didn't bother to greet Micky, but several of her friends giggled and did a quick change from pony to dog. 'Woofy-woofy-woof,' they chanted, paws up, barking in Micky's face.

'Silly twits,' said Micky, and he bared his teeth. 'Bitey-bitey-bite,' he said, snapping at Marigold's sore finger.

Marigold went red. The other girls giggled uncertainly, looking baffled.

'We don't want to play with my boring old brother,' said Marigold. 'Come on, we're all ponies and we've got to go in our stables now.'

They all galloped off towards the girls' toilets.

'Barmy lot,' said one of the girls in the top class.

'Not half,' said Micky.

She had a pocket chess set and started playing a game with one of the top class big boys. They didn't seem to mind Micky hanging around. The big boy was called Stuart and he had glasses and a lot of freckles. Micky was on his side, and he was pleased when he won. They began another game, and this time Stuart started telling Micky the names of all the chess pieces and showing him the moves they could make.

'Look, I can capture the White Queen now,' said Stuart.

'Well done,' said Micky, clapping Stuart on the back. Then he looked up and saw Darren and his gang approaching rapidly.

'*There* he is!' they shouted.

Micky swallowed. It looked like the Pink Boy's turn to be captured.

'I've got to go,' he gabbled to Stuart.

'OK. See you tomorrow lunchtime, eh? I'll teach you how to play properly if you like,' said Stuart.

'Great,' said Micky, and then he was up and running, with Darren and the gang baying at his heels.

He dodged round the little clumps of

children, making for the toilets, hoping he could get inside a cubicle and lock himself in. He collided with Marigold and her friends trotting out of the girls' toilets.

'There's Woofy-woofy-woof,' said one of them half-heartedly.

'Woofy-woofy-woof?' said Darren. 'Why do you keep calling him that?'

'Because he's scared of dogs,' she said.

'Scared of dogs!' said Darren, and he roared delightedly. 'Hear that, gang? Old Micky Mouse is scared of dogs.'

'No I'm not,' said Micky.

'Scared of little doggie-woggies?' said Darren, and he started growling and showing his teeth. 'Woofy-woofy-woof,' he went, copying the little girls.

'I'm not scared,' said Micky desperately.

'Cowardy little wimp. What sort of dogs you scared of, eh? Bet you're even scared of poxy old poodles and pekes. My dad's got a pit bull terrier and I'm not even scared of that, see,' said Darren. 'I'm not scared of anything.'

'I am,' said Micky. 'But not dogs.'

'Liar,' said Darren, and he caught hold of Micky and flicked his nose again. 'Let's get him, gang.'

'Yeah!'

'Fight! Fight! Fight!'

'Let's get out of here,' said Marigold's friends.

But Marigold stayed where she was. 'You leave my brother alone, you big bully,' she shouted. 'He's not scared of dogs, not any more.'

'Shut your face, Curly-nob,' said Darren, and he pushed Marigold out of the way.

It was a hard push and Marigold was still poised on tip-toe, being a pony. She was knocked off balance and fell back on to her bottom.

There was a roaring sound inside Micky's head. He prickled all over. He clenched his teeth.

'Don't push my sister around,' he said, and he punched Darren right in the nose.

It was only a very feeble punch, but Darren narrowed his eyes in fury and took aim. Micky saw Darren's huge bunched fist flying through the air towards him. But then there was a great howl and a growl and Wolfie came jumping right over the playground fence, rushing towards them, ears back, eyes gleaming, teeth snapping.

Darren's fist froze in mid-air. His mouth opened.

'Help!' he squeaked. 'He's coming for me!'

Darren was right. Wolfie practically flew through the air, snapping and slathering, aimed like a great grey dart at Darren's thick throat.

'A mad dog!'

'Get help!'

'It's going to get Darren!'

Darren burst into tears like a big baby.

'Help me, help me, help me,' he burbled.

'OK,' said Micky. 'Here, Wolfie. Good boy. Come here, pal.'

He snapped his fingers – and Wolfie swerved at the last minute and leapt up at Micky instead. He jumped into Micky's arms and licked his face lovingly, growling gruffly at this great game.

All the children in the playground stared, eyes wide, mouths gaping.

'I told you I'm not scared of dogs,' said Micky, giving Wolfie a big hug.

'Fancy Micky ...!'

'Isn't he *brave*.'

'And it was frothing at the mouth!'

'It nearly got Darren.'

'Look, Darren's still blubbing.'

'My brother Micky saved Darren.'

'Is it only a puppy? It looked so much bigger when it was running up to him.'

'What sort of dog is it, then?'

'They're all talking about us, Wolfie,' Micky whispered, nuzzling into him. 'So what are you doing here, boy?'

Mum came running into the playground, looking hot and flustered.

'Oh there he is! I thought I'd take him for a walk, but he suddenly bristled all over and went flying off ... I simply couldn't stop him. Bring him over here, Micky. What's he been up to? I've never known a dog get into so many scrapes.'

'You're not a boring old dog, are you,' Micky whispered into Wolfie's whiskery grey ear. 'You're my own special werepuppy – and we're going to get into lots and lots of scrapes together, aren't we, boy?'

Wolfie woofed delightedly. Micky looked deep into his glowing amber eyes and saw his own small face grinning happily back at him.